Atlas Moth

by Grace Hansen

Abdo
INCREDIBLE INSECTS
Kids

Abdo Kids Jumbo is an Imprint of Abdo Kids
abdobooks.com

abdobooks.com

Published by Abdo Kids, a division of ABDO, P.O. Box 398166, Minneapolis, Minnesota 55439. Copyright © 2022 by Abdo Consulting Group, Inc. International copyrights reserved in all countries. No part of this book may be reproduced in any form without written permission from the publisher. Abdo Kids Jumbo™ is a trademark and logo of Abdo Kids.

Printed in the United States of America, North Mankato, Minnesota.

052021

092021

THIS BOOK CONTAINS RECYCLED MATERIALS

Photo Credits: iStock, Shutterstock

Production Contributors: Teddy Borth, Jennie Forsberg, Grace Hansen
Design Contributors: Candice Keimig, Victoria Bates

Library of Congress Control Number: 2020947648
Publisher's Cataloging-in-Publication Data

Names: Hansen, Grace, author.

Title: Atlas moth / by Grace Hansen

Description: Minneapolis, Minnesota : Abdo Kids, 2022 | Series: Incredible insects | Includes online resources and index.

Identifiers: ISBN 9781098207359 (lib. bdg.) | ISBN 9781644945551 (pbk.) | ISBN 9781098208196 (ebook) | ISBN 9781098208615 (Read-to-Me ebook)

Subjects: LCSH: Attacus--Juvenile literature. | Moths--Juvenile literature. | Insects--Juvenile literature. | Insects--Behavior--Juvenile literature.

Classification: DDC 595.7--dc23

Table of Contents

Atlas Moths 4

Life Stages 14

More Facts 22

Glossary 23

Index 24

Abdo Kids Code 24

Atlas Moths

Atlas moths are native to Asia. They can be found in China, India, and other countries.

5

Atlas moths live in **tropical** dry forests and shrublands. As caterpillars, they can find lots of things to eat in these areas.

7

The atlas moth is one of the biggest insects in the world. Its **wingspan** can stretch more than 10 inches (25.4 cm)!

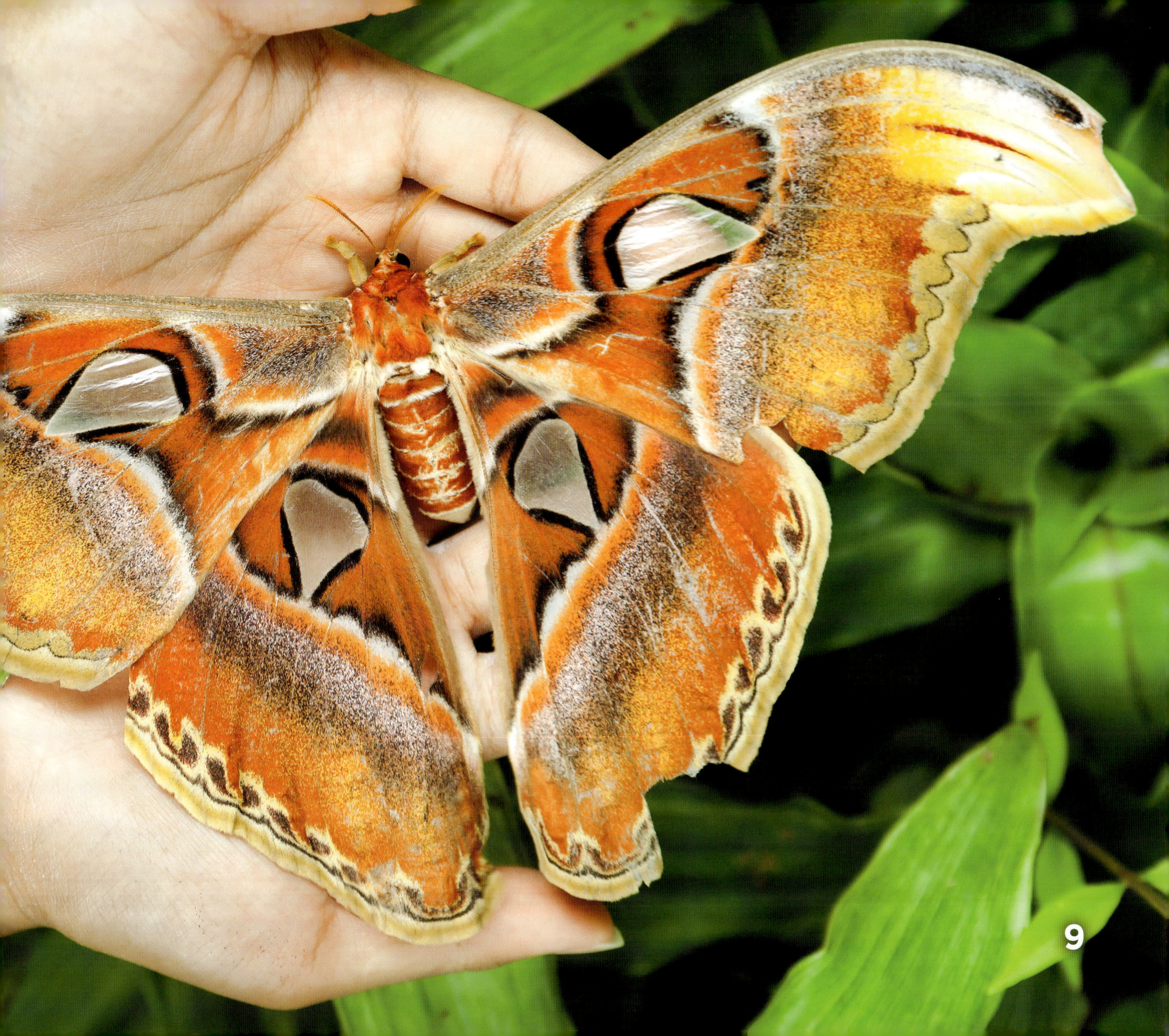

Atlas moths are so large that they spend most of their day resting. They have to save their energy in order to **mate**.

11

Atlas moths cannot get more energy from food. This is because they do not eat. They eat enough as caterpillars to **sustain** them.

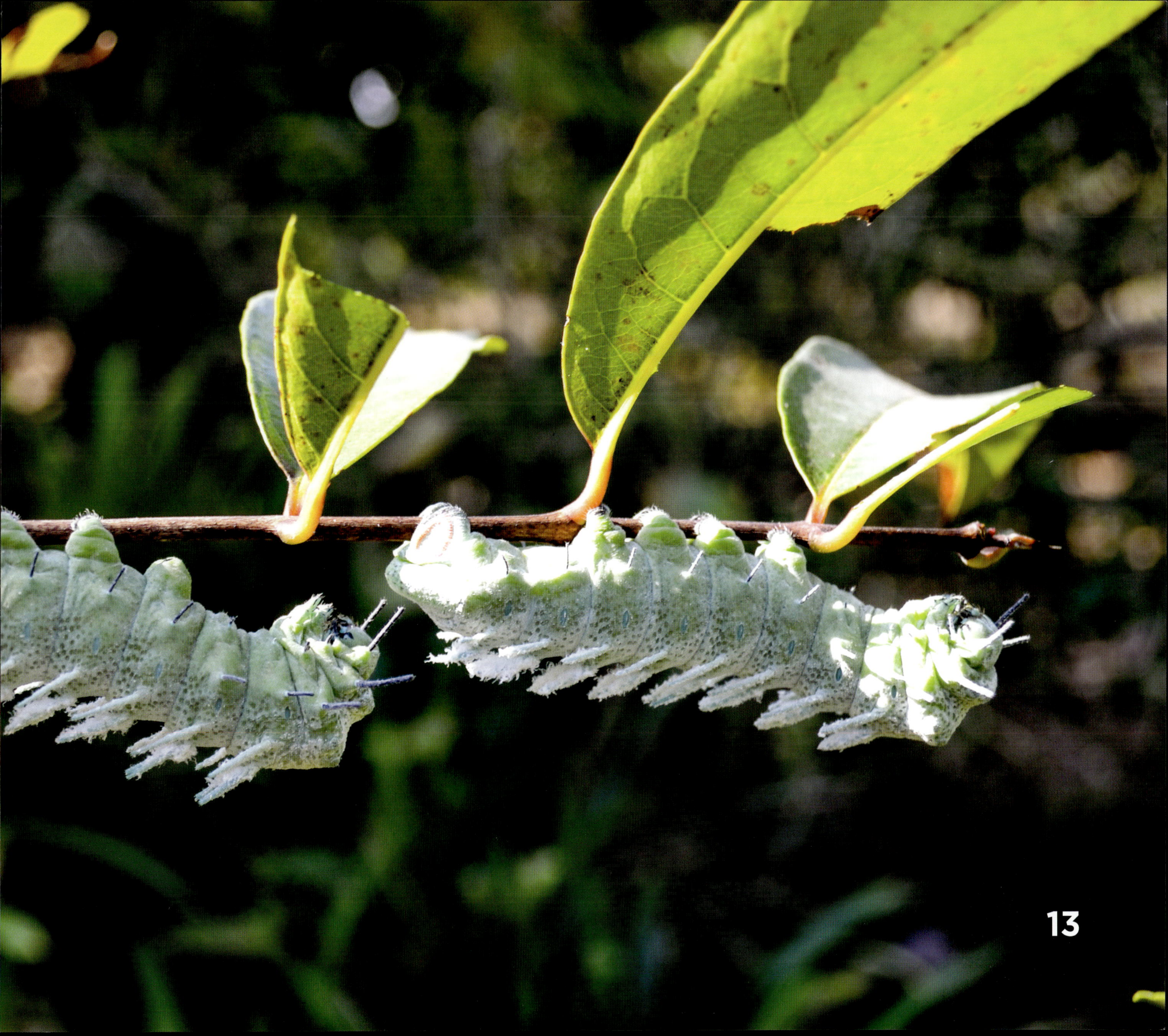

Life Stages

Atlas moth caterpillars, or larvae, hatch from eggs. The caterpillars eat the leaves of many plants. When they have eaten and grown enough, they are ready to **pupate**.

15

The caterpillars make a strong, brown silk. They use this to build their cocoons.

17

After about 4 weeks, the atlas moth breaks out of its cocoon. Its large wings open up to show a beautiful pattern.

19

The pattern on the wings is for more than just beauty. It can also scare away **predators**. The tips of the wings look like the heads of snakes!

21

More Facts

- Atlas moths are also found in Malaysia and Indonesia.

- Atlas moths only live for one to two weeks.

- In some places, people collect the used cocoons of Atlas moths. The cocoons are large and strong. They can be used as small purses.

Glossary

mate – to come together to have young.

native – belonging naturally to a place.

predator – an animal that hunts and eats other animals.

pupate – to become a pupa. A pupa is an inactive insect; the stage between larva and adult.

sustain – to provide with the basic necessities of life.

tropical – relating to the tropics, or areas near the equator that are warm all year round.

wingspan – the distance from the tip of one wing to the tip of the other.

Index

Asia 4

caterpillar 6, 12, 14, 16

China 4

cocoon 16, 18

defense 20

food 6, 12, 14

habitat 6

India 4

larvae 14

pupae 14

silk 16

size 8, 10

wings 8, 18, 20

wingspan 8

Visit **abdokids.com** to access crafts, games, videos, and more!

Use Abdo Kids code **IAK7359** or scan this QR code!